Thanks to Alain Douineau, Sophie Deschamps and Denis Larpin, Jardin des Plantes botanical garden, Paris

The illustrations in this book are created using gouache, coloured pencil and graphite.

Translated by Polly Lawson. First published in French as *La fête des fruits* by l'école des loisirs, Paris in 2017. First published in English by Floris Books, Edinburgh in 2018. This second edition 2022
 www.florisbooks.co.uk British Library CIP Data available ISBN 978-178250-804-5 Printed in Poland through Hussar

Floris Books supports sustainable forest management by printing this book on materials made from wood that comes from responsible sources and reclaimed material

How Does My Fruit Grow?

Gerda Muller

Floris Books

Sophie lived in a big city, but in the breaks from school she stayed with her Aunt Helen, Uncle Max and her big cousin Michael in the countryside.

When Michael arrived to pick her up at the beginning of the summer, Sophie was ready.

"Have a lovely time, darling," her mother said. "See you in two weeks."

strawberry, outside and inside

Picking berries

On Sophie's first morning at her uncle and aunt's house, Michael got out baskets, bowls and gardening gloves.

"The redcurrants and white currants are ready for picking," he said. "Can you fill these two bowls?"

"Of course," said Sophie, tasting a sour redcurrant.

"I'll tidy up the strawberry beds," said Michael, "and then we can pick them too. Do you know why strawberries are sometimes called 'false fruit'?"

"No," said Sophie, "why?"

"Well, inside each one of those redcurrants is a seed. But if you cut a strawberry in half, what do you see?"

"Hmm, not a single seed," puzzled Sophie.

Michael laughed, and decided to let Sophie find out for herself where strawberries grow their seeds.

(They're on the outside of the fruit!)

Cranberries

European cranberries grow on small shrub plants. American cranberries grow on a larger bush. Cranberries are too sour to eat raw, but they are often served as a sauce with meat, such as turkey or venison, and in America they are sweetened in pies and other desserts.

redcurrants white currants blackcurrants raspberries strawberries gooseberries

A party with a difference

"I have some friends coming over for a party this evening," said Michael. "A cherry party!"

He showed Sophie the trees covered with ripe cherries in the orchard. She thought the shiny red fruit looked delicious.

"Just don't eat the sour cherries on that tree over there," Michael warned. "They won't be ready until autumn and they're super-sour at the moment."

The two cousins spent the rest of the day getting ready. They collected six bowls full of cherries and hung lanterns in the trees.

"We'll light them when it gets dark," said Michael.

"They'll be like giant glowing cherries!" exclaimed Sophie happily.

When his friends arrived, Michael played his guitar and everyone sang. They ate big slices of pie – cherry pie, of course, baked by Aunt Helen.

It was a wonderful summer party!

This bird has eaten a cherry. The bird's stomach digests the cherry, and the cherry stone comes out onto the ground in the bird's droppings. Through the winter, the stone lies where it fell.

Then in spring a root sprouts and grows down into the soil. Soon a small seedling – a little cherry tree – starts growing upwards towards the sunlight. Cherry blossoms grow on the little tree.

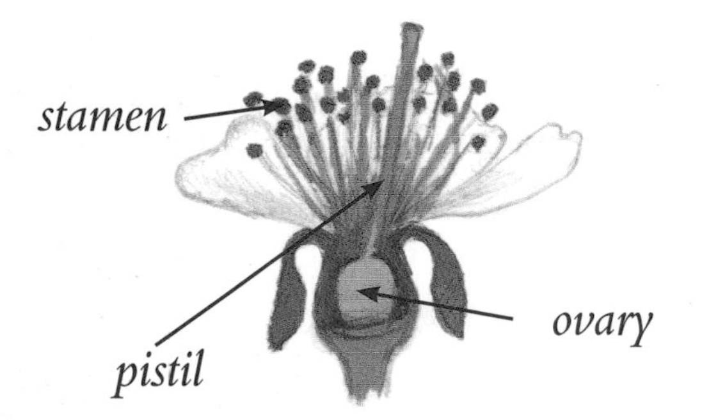

We wouldn't have cherries without bees.

When bees land on beautiful cherry blossom to collect nectar, pollen rubs off the stamen onto their fuzzy bodies. As the bees move from blossom to blossom, the pollen rubs onto the pistil. This fertilises the blossom's ovary, which then grows into a cherry fruit. Inside the cherry, a hard stone forms. What's inside the stone? Seeds to grow a new cherry tree.

Thank you, bees!

sweet cherries rainier cherries sour cherries in summer and in autumn

A surprise for Sophie

The next day, Michael took Sophie to the corner of the orchard where apples, pears, peaches and plums grew.

"Shake that little damson plum tree," he told Sophie, "and collect the fruit that falls off."

What a harvest! Sophie put fifteen damsons in her basket and ate the sixteenth, which was warm and sweet.

Michael wrapped pears on the pear tree in little bags, to protect the fruit from hungry insects. Then he used flowerpots to make homes for earwigs. "It's great having earwigs in the orchard," he explained, "because they eat nasty greenfly."

That evening, Sophie had an unexpected phone call from her father. He told her he had a new job in the south of France, and they were going to move house.

"I don't want to move so far away," sobbed Sophie.

Michael comforted her. "Don't be sad, Sophie," he said. "The south is beautiful and warm: lots of exciting plants grow there. We'll be in touch. And I know you'll make good new friends."

Apples

Apples have been eaten by humans throughout history, and were probably the first tree to be planted in orchards for fruit. Today there are around 7,500 varieties of apple grown around the world: so many that even experts have stopped using Latin names for them. Here are a few you might have tried:

King of the Pippins

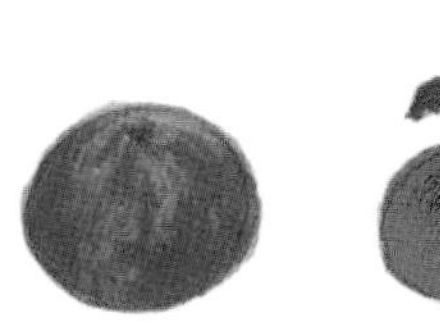

Royal Gala

Canadian Reinette

Belle de Boskoop

Red Delicious

Granny Smith

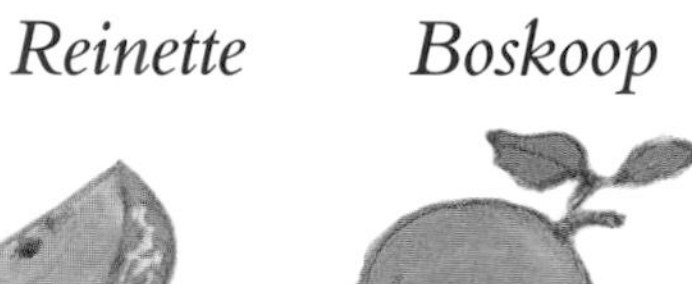

Golden Delicious

Gardeners plant passion-fruit vines for their spectacular flowers as well as their fruit.

Make a home for earwigs: fill an earthenware pot with straw. Wedge two small sticks across the straw so when the pot is turned upside down the straw doesn't fall out. Push a stake into the pot, then turn it all over so the pot hangs on the stake. Plant the stake in the ground near fruit trees.

earwig

pippin apple   peach   Williams or Bartlett pear   plums: greengages   mirabelles   damsons

A new friend

Back in the big city, Sophie found it hard to say goodbye to her classmates, her teacher and her home. She and her parents drove south behind the truck carrying all their furniture, and her mother tried to comfort her: "It feels sad, my darling. But think, our new house has a garden full of trees and vines."

When they arrived, Sophie spent the whole day carrying boxes into the house. Finally, she flopped down, tired out, under the pergola.

"Hello!" said a voice. "Welcome!" A girl, much older than Sophie, walked up the driveway to greet her. "My name's Manon," the girl went on, "and I live next door. Here, I've brought you some of our orange juice. What's your name?" Manon was very chatty. She said her parents were working in the olive grove behind their houses.

Sophie soon found she loved taking the bus each day with Manon, who was studying at the agricultural college. Manon's adopted brother, little Luc, was just starting school, so he went with them too.

Sophie wrote a letter to her old class:

Dear everyone,

When we arrived here, it felt like a faraway country. Everything is so different. The wind is hot and full of strange smells. There are pointy trees everywhere, like steeples.

The houses have small windows with shutters to keep out the sun, so it's cool inside.

I've made a friend already; she's eighteen and goes to college. She and I catch the same bus in the mornings. It's great!

I think of you all the time. Send me news!

Love,

Sophie

Kiwi

Kiwi fruit come from New Zealand but can be grown anywhere with a mild climate.

They are named after a large flightless bird that only lives in New Zealand and has feathers the same colour as the fuzzy kiwi-fruit skin. Kiwi fruit used to be called Chinese gooseberries until New Zealanders started selling them around the world and gave them a new name to tell people where they're from.

Even though the kiwi plant looks like a tree, it's actually a creeper and must be tied to a wall. The fruit ripen during autumn.

It's hot… very hot!

One evening, Manon and Luc came to see Sophie in her garden. They were carrying a large bucket.

"Your melons will be thirsty in this heat," said Manon. "We've brought them a big drink, which will do them good. Shall I water them?"

"Yes please," said Sophie. "Let me give you some apricots to say thank you."

They watched nearby grape pickers filling carts with fresh grapes.

"Those grapes will become wine," Manon explained. "The fruit will be crushed to make juice, which will be poured into barrels to ferment. When it is ready the wine makers will bottle the wine to sell in the shops."

In Sophie's garden there are also grapes growing, but Manon says they aren't for wine – they're delicious table grapes and are best eaten as soon as they're picked.

Sophie, Manon and little Luc go walking in dry rocky scrub to collect wild blueberries. "We'd better wash them before we eat them," said Manon. "Out here, a fox could have peed on them…"

kiwi fruit blueberries green and black grapes watermelon and other sweet melons apricots

pomegranate flower

quince flower

Some garden birds, like warblers, love eating figs. In fact in southern Europe some warblers are called fig-peckers.

In the south of France, pomegranate is juiced to make grenadine, a sweet syrup that is mixed with water. It makes a drink that is both sweet and tart. The word 'grenadine' comes from the French word for pomegranate: *grenades*. Grenadine bought in the supermarket is often made from pomegranate, blueberry, raspberry and strawberry juice, sweetened with sugar and sometimes flavoured with vanilla.

grenadine

So beautiful and so tasty!

On the day the figs were ready to harvest, Manon got up early to give Sophie's family a hand. She showed Sophie how to bend down the high branches with a special hooked stick.

"Today it's fig picking day," she said. "In the autumn, we'll harvest the quince. I love making quince jelly."

"When will the pomegranates be ready?" asked Sophie.

"Soon. We'll eat them fresh, or make grenadine with them."

"Will we make fig-adine from the figs?"

Manon laughed. "Oh, you're funny. No, we'll eat them fresh or dry them in the sun. Or cook up fig jam."

Sophie gave little Luc a hug. "Thanks for all your help," she said. "Take some figs home with you."

pomegranates
white fig
common fig
dried fig
quinces

The story of Noah comes from the Bible. It rained for forty days and forty nights until the earth was flooded. But God had asked Noah to build a huge ark, a boat that could keep every kind of animal and Noah's family safe from the flood.

When the rain stopped, a dove flew to the ark carrying an olive branch in its beak. This told Noah there was a tree nearby and so there must also be land. It was a symbol that God trusted the world and its people again.

How is olive oil made?
Black olives, including their stones, are crushed in a press. The 'juice' that runs off is a delicious and healthy oil used for cooking.

A long time ago, before electricity was discovered, people who lived near the Mediterranean Sea burned olive oil in lamps to make light. When archaeologists dig in old ruins, they often find these oil lamps.

The old olive tree

There was an old olive tree in Sophie's garden. One morning, Manon and her father came to harvest the green olives. They only picked some of the crop.

They leaned their ladders against the sturdy branches, and climbed up to reach the high olives. Manon gave Sophie a basket to collect some lower ones. "Don't eat them now," she said, "They only become delicious once they've been soaked in salty water. Your mother will soak the olives we're picking today and keep them in jars for eating."

"And what about all the olives you're leaving behind on the tree?" asked Sophie.

"Once they turn a beautiful shade of black, we do a second harvest," replied Manon. "Those olives are pressed to make olive oil." She climbed down. "Tomorrow we'll harvest the almonds."

"What about the persimmons," Sophie asked, nodding at the tree nearby. "When will they be ready?"

"The trees will lose their leaves," Manon told her. "But the fruit won't be ripe until the wintertime."

fragile almond blossom

almonds
green and black olives
persimmons

Grapefruit or pomelo?
A variety of grapefruit called a pomelo is becoming more popular. It's smaller and sweeter than a standard grapefruit.

The clementine was first grown by a monk, Brother Clement. It is a cross between a mandarin and a sweet orange: delicious! Clementines don't have pips, and are now much more common than mandarins.

Sophie's special corner

Sophie loved to sit under the orange tree in her garden and read, especially when the scent of its blossom filled the air. Nearby was a clementine tree, a lemon tree and, on the other side of the wall, a grapefruit tree.

"Let's pick the ripe oranges," said Manon one day.

"Good idea!" Sophie was delighted. They filled a basket, then ate their afternoon snack under the trees.

Sophie asked, "How old do you think this orange tree is?"

"I don't know," Manon replied, "but orange trees can live more than three hundred years."

"Three hundred?" cried little Luc. "As old as Grandpa?"

They all laughed.

"Which fruit tree lives the longest?" wondered Sophie.

Manon got out her tablet and typed the question. "It's the sweet chestnut," she reported. "They can live more than a thousand years. And some types of fruit have existed for a very long time. Apples are old, and plum stones have been found in prehistoric villages. People have eaten dates for more than seven thousand years."

"I'd love to know more about other times," said Sophie dreamily.

Melons have been eaten in Egypt for more than two and a half thousand years.

Pears have been eaten in China for more than six thousand years.

Many varieties of apple were eaten in Europe in the Middle Ages.

lemon and lime
orange
grapefruit and pink grapefruit
clementine

Brambles are from the same plant family as roses.

Autumn is here

Autumn arrived, and brought days of harvesting.

"Sophie, would you come with me to gather a friend's walnuts tomorrow?" asked Manon. "We have to knock them down from the trees with a long pole."

"I'd love to," said Sophie, "but what if the poles are too heavy for me?"

"We'll find one the right size," promised Manon. "You can do the lower branches."

Manon's friend was very happy to have so much help.

Sophie has made a brown paint from walnut husks.

After they'd harvested the walnuts Sophie and Manon discovered bramble bushes that were covered in wild blackberries. Sophie decided the wild ones were much tastier than the cultivated blackberries in her garden. The hazelnut trees around them were laden too. The girls saw all sorts of creatures were enjoying the nuts.

The blackberries in Sophie's garden grow on bushes without thorns. The berries hang in little clusters, and are easy to harvest.

In olden days, people thought that walnut trees were enchanted, because no other plants ever grew near them. Nowadays we know that walnut leaves contain a toxin, and when it rains the toxin washes into the soil so other plants can't grow there.

walnut husk, shell and kernel | garden blackberries | wild blackberries | hazelnuts

Thank you, sweet chestnuts!

Sweet chestnut trees flower in spring. The flowers are long, pretty catkins.

Sophie's father had a friend called Thomas, who lived in the low hills nearby in the middle of a chestnut wood. The spiky chestnut burrs were ripening and falling to the ground, so Sophie, Manon and Sophie's father went to help with the harvest.

"Long ago, poor peasants around here made flour from the chestnuts, and used it to bake bread and thicken soup," Thomas told them as they worked. "Without the chestnuts, they would have starved."

"That sounds hard," said Sophie. "Thank you, chestnut trees!"

They each had gloves, a bucket and a small wooden tool for tapping the chestnut burrs to split them open. Once a burr cracked, the nuts came out easily and no one's hands got spiked. Manon and Sophie enjoyed the harvest and quickly filled their buckets with shiny chestnuts.

Horse chestnut trees also have very pretty white or pink flowers grouped in cone shapes, but the horse chestnuts themselves (which are sometimes called conkers) are poisonous. They're not for eating; instead, children often play games with them.

Back at home, Sophie's father roasted some of the chestnuts they'd collected. He cut a slit in each hard shell first so they didn't explode. Sophie carefully fanned the flames under the cast-iron chestnut pan. The smell was wonderful!

Hot sweet chestnuts are a delicious market treat in late autumn.

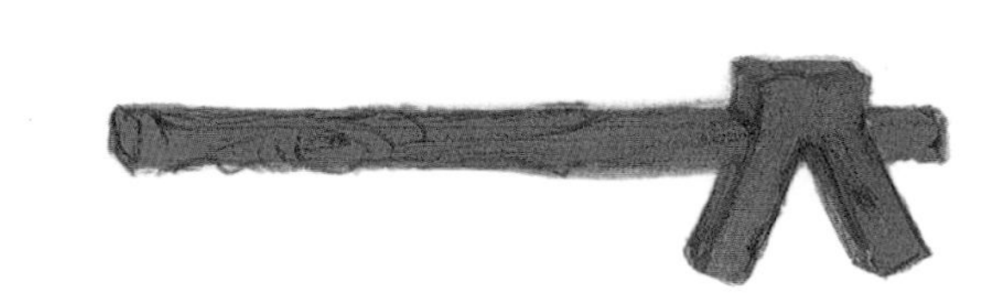

This little wooden tool is used by chestnut harvesters to split open the spiky husk.

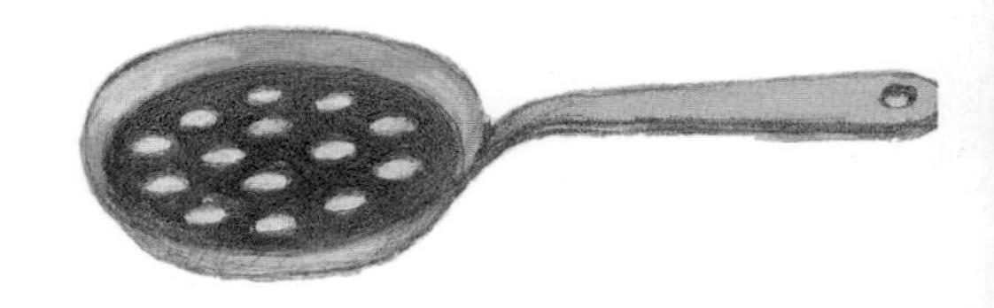

A cast-iron pan or skillet for roasting chestnuts.

chestnut burr in summer
chestnuts in autumn in their husk
chestnuts
hot roasted chestnut

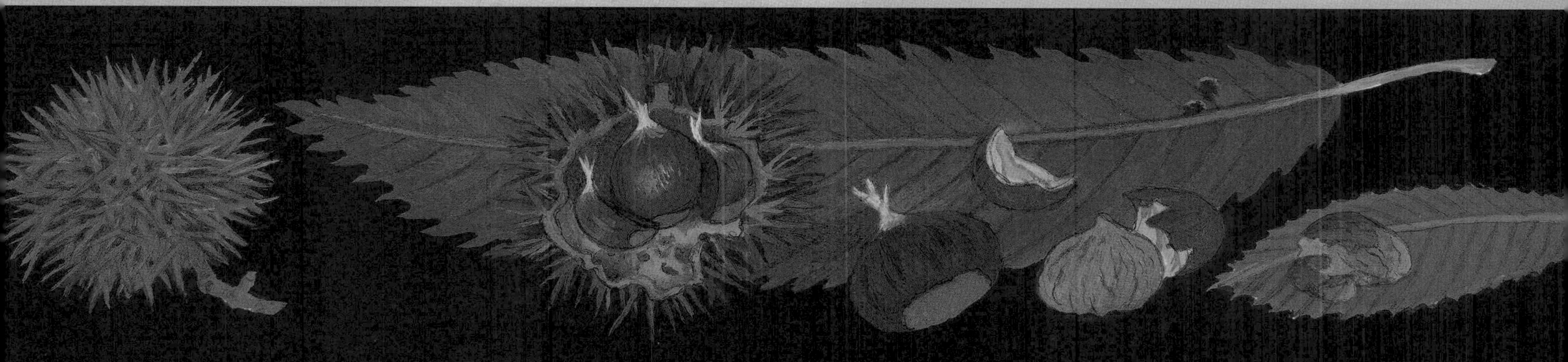

A wonderful idea

By now, Sophie was feeling very settled in her new home and she loved her new school. Her teacher was kind and had lots of good ideas. One morning, the teacher asked the children what their favourite fruit was.

"Mango!"

"Prickly pear!"

"Bananas!"

They all shouted at once.

"And do you know how these tropical fruits grow?" asked the teacher.

"Mangos must grow like tomatoes, tied to a stake," said Tristan confidently.

"I think bananas grow in bunches like cherries," suggested Magalie.

"I know!" cried Martin. "Prickly pears hang from trees."

The teacher laughed. "Great guesses! But not quite." She smiled. "That settles it. We're going to create a big presentation. We'll call it: How Does Our Fruit Grow? It will be about the tropical fruit we buy in our supermarkets. Mr Mathieux, your art teacher, will draw pictures of the fruits, then you can paint them.

And you're going to research and write all the information to go next to the pictures. Here are some books and magazines to read. Let's see what we can find out!"

They read, they typed, they printed out words and they painted the drawings. At last all their work was on display in the school hall.

Lychee

In the low mountains of China, where I come from, there are more than a hundred varieties of lychee! I love picking them and eating them raw, all juicy. My little brother likes them best when they're dried, swimming in syrup. LÉLÉ

Mango

The world would be a sadder place without mangos! Mangos grow everywhere in hot countries: in big orchards and also in small gardens. The fruit's skin is orange, or red and green, and inside it is succulent and juicy. Perfect for eating fresh, or making chutney or juice or mango ice cream.

Maï

Passion fruit

The passion fruit is the only fruit in the passion vines family that you can eat. Inside its thick skin, the flesh is juicy and it smells sweet and tropical.

Marc

Dates

Date palms grow in very hot countries where there isn't much rain, but they can also cope with a little frost. You find a group of them in a desert oasis, where there is water under the sand. There is an Arab saying: date palms like to have 'their head in the fire of the sky and their feet in the water'.

You can eat dates fresh or dried; some are big, some are small.

To pick dates, you have to climb the tree trunk wearing spiked shoes, and carrying a rope and a knife. You fasten a bunch of dates to the rope and lower it to the ground. Someone on the ground unties the dates, and you pull the rope back up for the next bunch.

Hocine

bunch of small dates fresh dates dried dates candied dates

Coconut

Every part of the coconut is useful! You can drink coconut milk when you're thirsty, eat solid coconut when you're hungry and burn coconut shells to make a fire to cook food on. You can even weave coconut palm leaves into baskets.

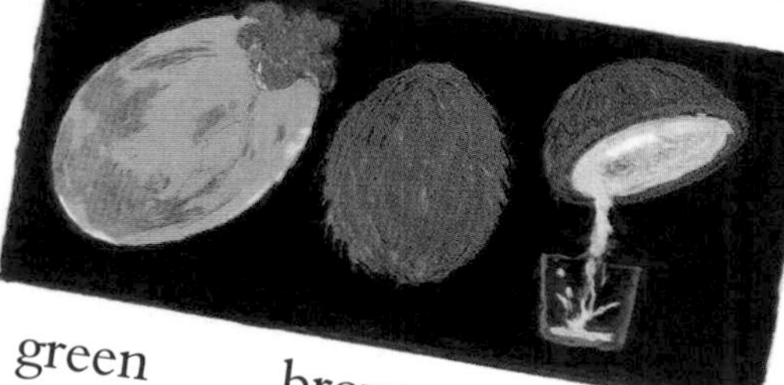

green husk

brown, fibrous shell

coconut milk

It's said that coconut palms love the sound of the sea. Floating coconuts can travel a long way across the ocean before washing up on a beach and growing a new palm tree.

Camille

Papaya

The papaya tree isn't really a tree, because its trunk is actually made of leaves. The leaves have formed into a solid base. The papaya tree doesn't have branches either; instead it has big leaves on the end of long stems. The fruits grow directly on the leafy trunk. A milky fluid (latex) flows through the plant, and is very good for cleaning wounds.

In Mexico, my grandmother used latex when I hurt myself, and so did the doctors.

papaya

papaya cut in half

Valentina

Banana

This is the banana plant. They grow in places that are hot all year round. They are huge plants. The way they grow is that young leaves sprout from a big bulb in the ground called a corm. The leaves grow big and long, then form together in a solid trunk, which is sometimes called a 'false stem'. After that, a flower spike grows inside the trunk, coming out the top.

Bats often fertilise banana flowers when they're searching for nectar. The flowers develop into bunches of fruit. The spike bends down, pulled by the weight of the bananas.

Bananas are cut off the plant when they're still green, and the rest of the plant is cut down too! But it re-grows very quickly because it already has offshoots.

Giant banana leaves can be used as umbrellas, or even to make a roof. They're also helpful in cooking and can be used as a big serving plate.

Sophie

banana corm with young leaves sprouting

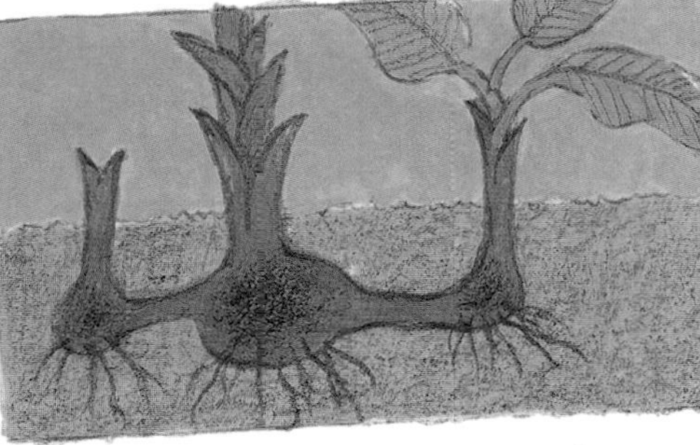

new offshoots from the corm underground

green and yellow bananas

Did you know nuts are a kind of fruit?

Here are four dried fruits we eat as snacks

Pecan or hickory

leaves shell kernel

The pecan tree is related to European nut trees but needs a warmer climate to produce fruit. Inside a pecan's smooth shell is a delicious kernel, rich in energy. Pecans are harvested with a long stick, like walnuts.

Stef

Pistachio

The outside of the pistachio fruit is hard and pink, but inside, the seed is green. This is the pistachio nut. I do like eating them raw, but they're even better when they're toasted over a fire. When I was on holiday in Greece, my grandmother baked me a delicious pistachio cake.

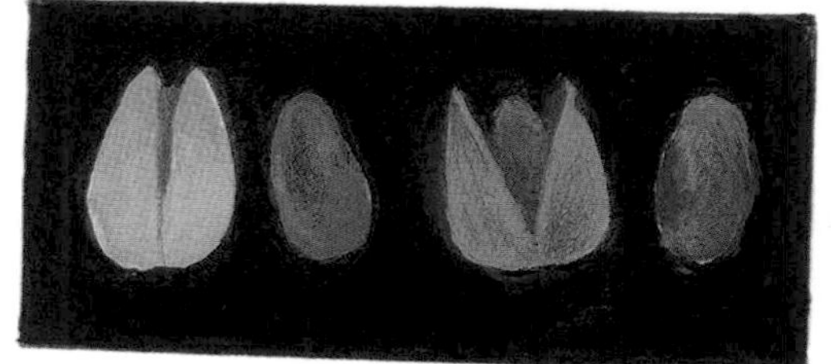

YANNIS

Peanuts

The peanut plant has flowers that wilt towards the ground.

The flowers push slowly into the soil, where they transform into peanuts.

Peanut plants came from South America. We often buy peanuts already shelled and roasted.

Claire

Cashew

The nut of the cashew grows hanging underneath the cashew apple, a sweet, juicy, red fruit. The nut is kidney-shaped, and is eaten raw or roasted. It's covered in a thick skin. Warning! Cashew skin contains an irritant, which can hurt you. If you're working with cashews you have to wear thick gloves. Cashew shelling and roasting is difficult, careful work.

I love cashews, especially roasted.

Neelan

Prickly pear

These juicy fruits are also known as Barbary figs, which would suggest they come from the North African Barbary Coast, but in fact they are originally from Mexico. They grow on spiny cactus 'paddles', the flat branches of cactuses. They're farmed in hot countries, but also grow in the wild.

The prickly pear fruit is covered in tiny bristles, so you need to wear gloves when you're peeling them.

Antoine

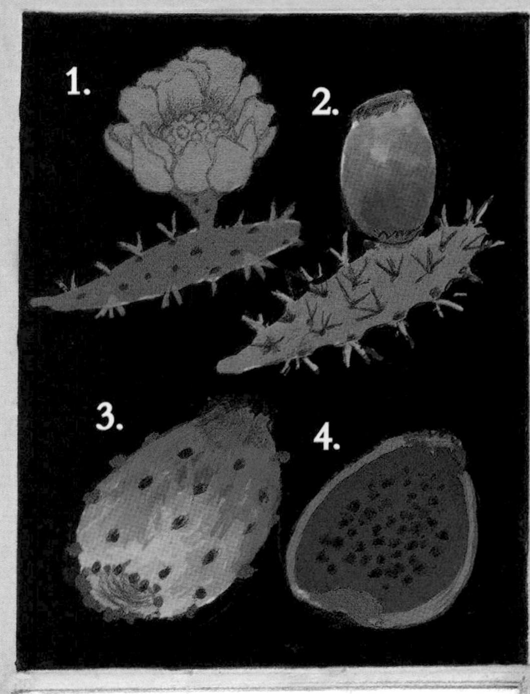

1. flower
2. prickly pear growing
3. whole prickly pear
4. inside the fruit

Kumquat

Happily the kumquat, originally from China, grows on a bush, so it's easy to harvest these little fruits. You eat them whole: the skin of the kumquat is sweeter than the flesh! They also make good marmalade. *Anne*

kumquat fruits

Presentation day!

Finally the day of the presentation arrived. The children's families and friends wandered around the school hall looking at all the display boards and tasting the fresh fruit and fruit juice. Everyone thought the presentation was wonderful!

By the time Sophie and her parents got home, it was dark. "What a great evening," her father said. "Now it's past bedtime. Sleep tight, sweetheart."

But Sophie wasn't tired, she sat at her window looking out at the stars, the lights of the town, the hills and the fields. "I've learnt so much this year," she thought happily. "One day, I'll go and explore on the other side of those hills and find out more and more!"

Before fruit can grow, there has to be a flower.

peanuts

hazelnuts

prickly pears

quince

chestnuts

bananas

Gerda Muller is a renowned European illustrator and author. Born in 1926 in the Netherlands, Gerda has lived in Paris for most of her working life. She has created more than 120 children's books; most have been translated into multiple languages.

Gerda's greatest inspiration is her love of nature, and her picture books are treasured for their vibrant and detailed illustrations of the natural world.

"When I work alone in my studio, I feel the presence of a child who looks and often guides me; it is for that child that I work – not for parents or for publishers." – Gerda Muller